A Note to Parents

For many children, learning math is difficult and "I hate math!" is their first response — to which many parents silently add "Me, too!" Children often see adults comfortably reading and writing, but they rarely have such models for mathematics. And math fear can be catching!

The easy-to-read stories in this **Hello Reader! Math** series were written to give children a positive introduction to mathematics, and parents a pleasurable re-acquaintance with a subject that is important to everyone's life. **Hello Reader! Math** stories make mathematical ideas accessible, interesting, and fun for children. The activities and suggestions at the end of each book provide parents with a hands-on approach to help children develop mathematical interest and confidence.

Enjoy the mathematics!

• Give your child a chance to retell the story. The more familiar children are with the story, the more they will understand its mathematical concepts.
• Use the colorful illustrations to help children "hear and see" the math at work in the story.
• Treat the math activities as games to be played for fun. Follow your child's lead. Spend time on those activities that engage your child's interest and curiosity.
• Activities, especially ones using physical materials, help make abstract mathematical ideas concrete.

Learning is a messy process. Learning about math calls for children to become immersed in lively experiences that help them make sense of mathematical concepts and symbols.

Although learning about numbers is basic to math, other ideas, such as identifying shapes and patterns, measuring, collecting and interpreting data, reasoning logically, and thinking about chance, are also important. By reading these stories and having fun with the activities, you will help your child enthusiastically say "**Hello, math,**" instead of "I hate math."

—Marilyn Burns
National Mathematics Educator
Author of *The I Hate Mathematics! Book*

For my big sister Judy,
who always shared her money
— T.S.

To Kathryn
—A.L.

Copyright © 1998 by Scholastic Inc.
The activities on pages 44-48 copyright © 1998 by Marilyn Burns.
All rights reserved. Published by Scholastic Inc.
SCHOLASTIC, HELLO READER! and CARTWHEEL BOOKS
and associated logos are trademarks and/or registered trademarks
of Scholastic Inc.

Library of Congress Cataloging-in-Publication Data

Slater, Teddy.
    Max's money / by Teddy Slater; illustrated by Anthony Lewis.
        p.   cm.—(Hello reader! Math. Level 4)
    Summary: Max finds out about adding and subtracting different amounts of money as he tries to borrow or earn enough to buy a birthday present for his mother. Includes related activities.
    ISBN 0-590-12010-7
    [1. Money—Fiction.]   I. Lewis, Anthony, 1966-   ill.   II. Title.
III. Series.
PZ7.S6294Max   1998
[Fic]—dc21
                                                                98-23333
                                                                    CIP
                                                                    AC

Library of Congress Cataloging-in-Publication Data

15 14 13 12 11 10 9 8   7 8 9 10/0

Printed in the U.S.A.
First printing, December 1998

Max's Money

by Teddy Slater
Illustrated by Anthony Lewis
Math Activities by Marilyn Burns

Hello Reader! Math — Level 4

SCHOLASTIC INC.
New York Toronto London Auckland Sydney

Chapter One:
It's the Thought That Counts

A big KEEP OUT sign was hanging outside my sister Sophie's room. I pressed my ear to the door and tried to figure out what was going on inside.

ZIP!

RIP!

SNIP!

It sounded interesting.

I bent down and peeked through the keyhole. But there wasn't much to see. It looked as if the room was empty.

I pushed the door open and walked right in.

My sister was sitting on the floor in the middle of a mess. There was lots of shiny gold paper, a roll of red ribbon, sticky tape, scissors, and a big cardboard box.

"Close the door," Sophie said. "I'm wrapping Mom's present. I don't want her to see."

"What is it?" I asked.

Sophie opened the box and pulled out a pair of pink fuzzy slippers.

"What did *you* get her?" Sophie asked.

"Nothing yet," I admitted. "I don't know what to get."

"Well, you have to decide soon," Sophie said. "Mom's birthday is only a week away."

"Don't worry," I said. "I'll think of something."

That night at dinner, everyone was talking about Mom's birthday.

"I'm going to cook you the best birthday feast ever," Dad told Mom.

"I'm going to give you the best birthday hug," my little brother Timmy said.

"My present is a surprise," Sophie announced.

"Mine, too," my big brothers Peter and Will said together.

"Hey, Mom's birthday is still a week away," I reminded everyone.

"I can hardly wait," Mom said with a smile.
"But I don't want you kids to spend a lot of
money on me," she added. "Remember, it's the
thought that counts — not the gift."

Boy! Was I glad to hear her say that.
I didn't have a lot of money!

It was Will's turn to do the dishes. So after dinner I went straight to my room.

I picked up my piggy bank. It felt heavier than I remembered. I could tell there was lots of money inside.

But when I emptied it onto my bed, it was mostly just pennies.

I stacked the coins on my desk and groaned.
There were 47 pennies, 6 nickels,
3 dimes, and 1 quarter. It wasn't even
enough for a fancy birthday card.

I looked in all the pockets of all my clothes
and dug up 3 more pennies and another dime.

I went down to the den and searched between the sofa cushions. Some change always falls out of Dad's pockets when he naps there.

Our family has a rule about that sofa — Finders Keepers! This time I found 1 nickel and 2 quarters.

Now I had $2. It still wasn't much. But it was better than nothing.

Chapter Two: Money Matters

The next day was Saturday. I got up early and rode my bike to Main Street.

I looked in all the store windows. There was lots of stuff to see.

Some of it was really nice. And really expensive.

Some of it was really ugly. And still expensive.

But even the cheapest things cost a lot more money than I had.

And then I saw the perfect present!

$ 4 · 99

It cost too much, too.

There was only one thing to do. I got back on my bike and pedaled home.

I counted my money again and put it back in my piggy bank. Then I went to look for my dad.

He was in the garden watering the strawberries.

"Hey, Dad," I said. "Can I have an advance on my allowance?"

"Don't tell me you want to buy more baseball cards," Dad said.

"Not this time," I said. "I need the money for Mom's birthday present."

"Sorry, Max," Dad said. "I could give you the money for Mom's gift. But then the gift would be from me. It wouldn't be from you."

"You don't have to give me the money," I said. "Just lend it."

"Sorry, Max," Dad said again. Then he picked a huge red strawberry and handed it to me.

"Not all gifts cost money," he said. "Use your imagination, Max. You'll think of something."

I thought and I thought. But all I could think
of was the pin. I knew Mom would love it.

I already had two dollars of my own. If
Sophie, Peter, and Will each lent me one dollar,
I would have enough to buy the pin.

I decided to ask my sister first. Sophie is the oldest. The richest, too. My allowance is only a dollar and a quarter a week. Sophie gets four times as much. And she earns even more babysitting.

I went upstairs to Sophie's room. This time the door was wide open.

"I know what I'm getting Mom for her birthday," I told Sophie.

"What is it?" she asked.

"A pin," I answered. "It's shaped like a heart and it looks just like real gold."

"That sounds wonderful," Sophie said. "Mom will love it."

"There's only one problem," I said. "I need to borrow a dollar."

"Not from me!" Sophie laughed. "You already owe me two dollars!"

"Come on, Sis," I pleaded. "I promise to pay you back."

"Sorry, Max," she said. "I don't think Mom would want you to spend all your money on her. And I know she wouldn't want you to spend mine!"

I could tell there was no point arguing.
So I went next door to Peter's room.

I had to ask him for two dollars — to make
up for the one Sophie didn't lend me.

"Are you kidding?" Peter exclaimed. "Do you
have any idea how much you already owe me?"

Peter went to his desk and picked up a sheet of paper. It had a whole bunch of dates and numbers written on it.

Uh-oh! I had a feeling Peter was going to answer his own question.

"This much!" he said, pointing to the numbers.

"Never mind," I said. What else could I say?

I headed down the hall to Will's room. But I wasn't very hopeful. Now I would have to ask him for the whole three dollars.

Will has almost as much money as Sophie. That's because he never spends his whole allowance. He saves it!

Will hardly ever buys anything. And he never ever lends any money to anybody.

Will and Timmy were playing Go Fish in Will's room.

"Will," I said. "I need three dollars to buy —"

"No!" Will said. He didn't even let me finish my sentence.

But Timmy jumped up and ran out of the room. A minute later, he was back. He was holding a fistful of paper play money.

Timmy shoved the bills into my hand.

"Here, Max," he said. "You can have all my money."

Timmy is a great little kid. But he doesn't have a clue about money. I gave him a big hug anyway. "Thanks, pal," I said. "You're the best."

Then I tried Will again. "Come on," I begged. "I really need the money for Mom's birthday gift."

"If you need money, you should get a job," Will said.

"I'm only eight years old," I pointed out. "Who would hire me?"

Will looked at me. Then he looked at his room. The bed was covered with dirty laundry. The floor was covered with toys. There were a million dust bunnies under his desk and a billion papers on top of it.

"I will hire you!" Will said. "I'll pay you a dollar to sort my laundry, 50 cents to put away all my other junk, 35 cents to clean my desk, and 45 cents to vacuum the floor."

"Are you kidding?" I said.

Will took another look at the room. "No," he said. "I'm serious."

I wrote the numbers down and added them up.

"It isn't enough," I said. "I told you I need three dollars."

"Okay," Will said. "I'll give you another 20 cents a day to make my bed. Is it a deal?"

I added the money again. It was even more than I needed.

"It's a deal!" I said.

Chapter Three:
Working for Will

I went to work the very next morning.
First I sorted all the clothes into two big piles—

CLEAN   and   DIRTY.

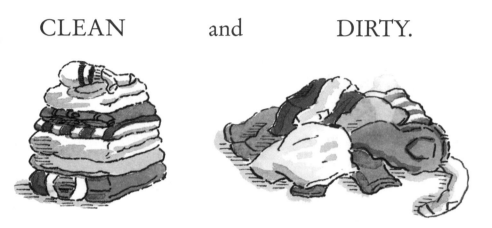

Then I put all the toys in the toy box.

When everything was off the floor, I
vacuumed the rug.

Will looked around the room and smiled.
"Good job, Max!" he said.

I made Will's bed every day for the next six days.

By the sixth day, the rest of the room was a mess again. But the bed looked great.

"Pay up!" I told Will.

Will reached into his pocket. He pulled out two dollar bills, three quarters, three nickels, and six dimes.

Will put the money on top of his desk. I picked it up and counted it.

Exactly $3.50.

Just then, Sophie came into the room.

"Whose money is that?" she asked.

"It's mine," I said.

My sister plucked 1 dollar bill, 2 quarters, and 5 dimes right out of my hand.

"The rest of it may be yours," she said, "but this is mine! Now you don't owe me any more money."

"Me either," someone else said.

I looked up, and there was Peter.

He reached out and took 1 quarter, 1 dime, 2 nickels, and the other dollar.

I looked down at my hand. There was only a nickel left.

Rats!

Chapter Four:
The Perfect Present

I went back to my room and emptied out my piggy bank. I added that money to the nickel and biked back to Main Street.

I rode past the nice expensive stuff.

Past the ugly expensive stuff.

Past the perfect pin.

I went into the card store.

And there I found the perfect card.

It only cost $2! (So I had a nickel left over for gum.)

The card was blank on the inside. I took it home and tried to think of the perfect thing to write on it.

I thought and I thought.

Then I started to write.

The next day was Mom's birthday.

She loved the special dinner Dad cooked for her.

We all did.

There were big juicy lamb chops, little green peas, fluffy mashed potatoes, and a super-gooey birthday cake.

After she blew out the candles, we all gave Mom her presents.

Sophie gave her the fuzzy slippers.

Peter gave her perfume.

Will gave her a silky scarf.

Timmy gave her a big red balloon.

I gave her the card.

ROSES ARE RED
VIOLETS ARE BLUE
I DON'T HAVE LOTS OF MONEY
BUT I REALLY DO LOVE YOU!
Happy Birthday to the best
Mom in the whole
Wide world.
Love and kisses,
Max

Mom put Sophie's slippers on her feet and tied Will's scarf around her neck.

She dabbed Peter's perfume behind her ears.

She tied Timmy's balloon to the refrigerator handle, and she stuck my card on the door.

Then Mom went around the table and gave each of us a big hug and a kiss.

"This has been the most perfect birthday I ever had," she said with a grin.

We all grinned back. That's what she says every year.

But this time I could tell she really, really meant it.

• ABOUT THE ACTIVITIES •

Learning about money is a basic, real-world skill. Children need to learn the names of coins, how much each is worth, and how to figure out the value of collections of coins. Learning about our monetary system is also extremely valuable for developing and honing children's number sense and ability to compute. Figuring out how much a dime and four nickels are worth all together, for example, requires that a child compute how much four nickels are worth and also add on 10 cents. Doing this figuring helps with addition, multiplication, and mental computation.

Children best learn about money from having many opportunities to use money in real-world and play situations. The activities and games in this section provide children with valuable first-hand experiences. Before doing them, assemble a collection of coins — 6 quarters, 10 dimes, 10 nickels, and 50 pennies — and also have two dollar bills on hand. Then enjoy the activities with your child!

— Marilyn Burns

You'll find tips and suggestions for guiding the activities whenever you see a box like this!

Chapter One
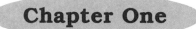

Max empties out his piggy bank and finds 47 pennies, 6 nickels, 3 dimes, and 1 quarter. How much money was in his bank?

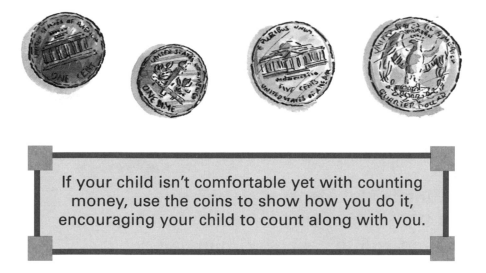

> If your child isn't comfortable yet with counting money, use the coins to show how you do it, encouraging your child to count along with you.

Max finds 3 more pennies and 1 dime in his pockets. How much money did he have now?

Max searched in the sofa and found 1 nickel and 2 quarters. How much money did he find? Now he thought he had $2.00. Can you explain how Max figured?

> It's important to remember that there is more than one way to count up coins. Encourage your child to explain out loud how he or she figures.

Chapter Two

On Main Street, Max saw a  for $100.

But Max only had $2.00. How much more money did he need to buy it?

Then he saw a for $150. How much more money did Max need to buy this?

Then he saw a for $75 and a for $50. How much more money did Max need to buy each of these?

Finally Max decided to buy a for $4.99. Explain why he wants to ask Sophie, Peter, and Will to each lend him one dollar.

Max's allowance is a dollar and a quarter a week, but Sophie gets four times as much. How much allowance does Sophie get?

Then Max asked Will. Will wouldn't lend Max money either, but he offered him a job. Will said he'd pay a dollar for sorting his laundry, 50 cents for putting away his junk, 35 cents for cleaning his desk, and 45 cents for vacuuming. How much would Max earn for doing these chores?

Will also agreed to pay Max 20 cents a day for making his bed. How much would Max earn if he made Will's bed for six days?

Chapter Three

After six days, Will paid Max $3.50. But then Sophie came to collect what Max owed her. She took 1 dollar bill, 2 quarters, and 5 dimes. How much did Sophie take? How much money did Max have left?

Then Peter took the money Max owed him — 1 quarter, 1 dime, 2 nickels, and a dollar bill. How much did Peter take? How much did Max have left?

Chapter Four

Max took the nickel and the $2.00 from his piggy bank. How much did he have all together now?

No Peeking

You need a collection of coins in a paper bag. Name an amount that is less that one dollar, like 0 cents or 67 cents. Then, without peeking, reach into the bag and pick out coins, one by one, until you get to the amount you named EXACTLY. If you go over the exact amount, you can put back any coin you'd like, reach in, and take out another.

Race for $1.00

This is a game for two people. You need a collection of coins, a $1.00 bill, and one die.

When it's your turn, roll the die. The number that comes up tells you the amount of money to take. (1 means one cent, 2 means two cents, etc.) Also on your turn, you can exchange any of the coins you have for others as long as you keep the amount the same. For example, you can exchange 10 pennies for a dime, or two dimes and a nickel for a quarter. When you're finished exchanging, pass the die to the other player.

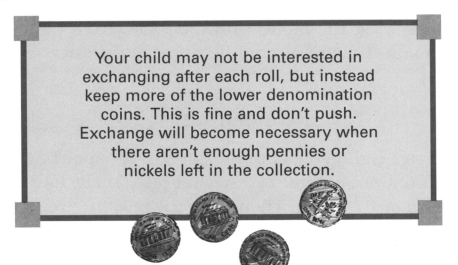

Your child may not be interested in exchanging after each roll, but instead keep more of the lower denomination coins. This is fine and don't push. Exchange will become necessary when there aren't enough pennies or nickels left in the collection.

Another way to play Race for $1.00 is to roll two dice instead of one. Try it. Which way do you like better?